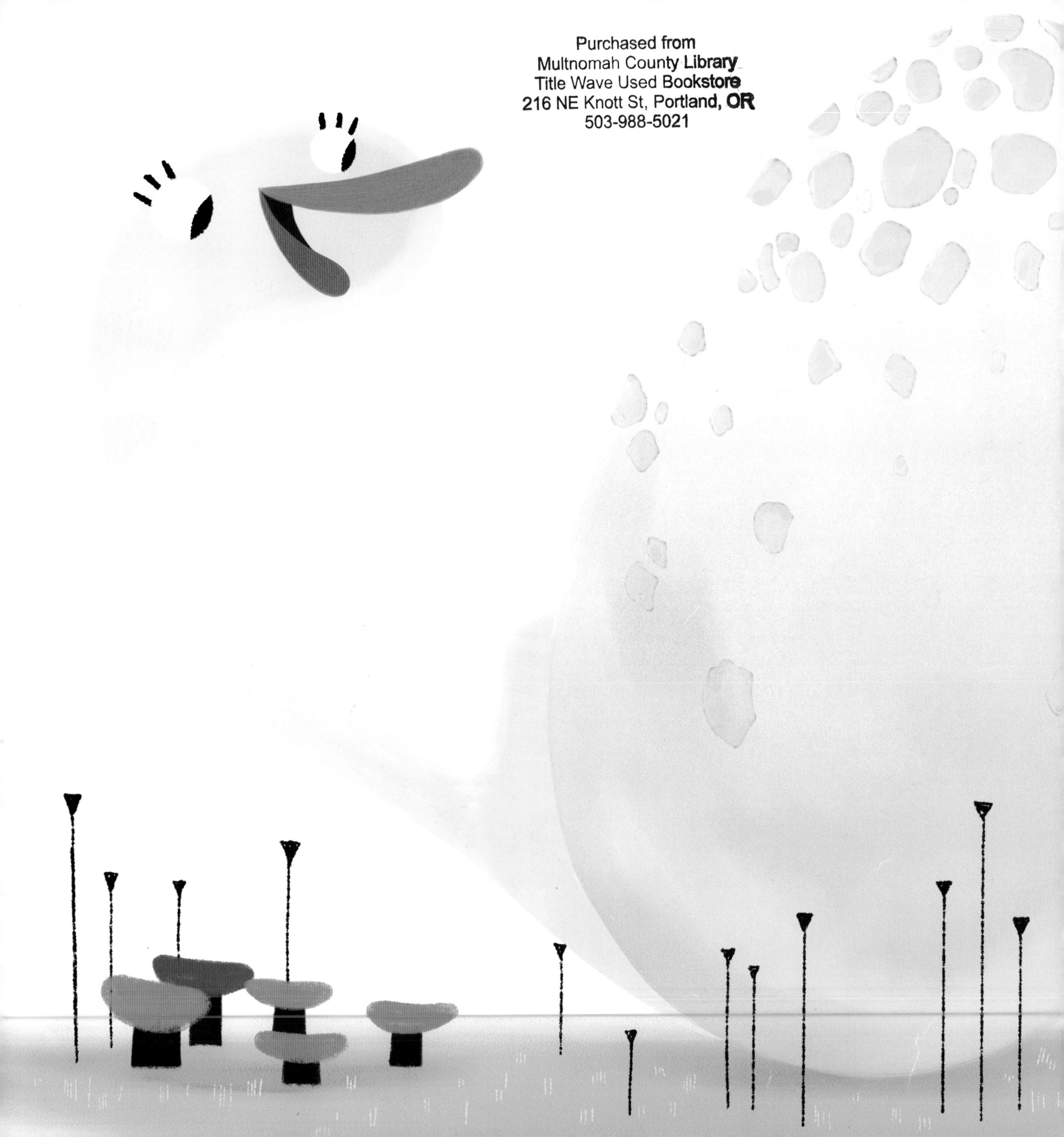

DUCK, DUCK, DINOSAUR

KALLIE GEORGE · Illustrated by ORIOL VIDAL

HARPER

An Imprint of HarperCollinsPublishers

To my husband,
who loves dinosaurs —K.G.

To my family,
the best family —O.V.

ISBN 978-0-06-235308-5
The artist used a tablet to create the digital illustrations for this book.
Typography by Joe Merkel
15 16 17 18 19 SCP 10 9 8 7 6 5 4 3 2 1
❖
First Edition

Mama Duck's eggs hadn't hatched yet,
but already she felt like the luckiest duck in the pond.
Soon she would have a big, happy family.

DUCKS

At last one egg began to wiggle.
It wiggled and wobbled, and then . . .

CRACK!

Out hatched a very fluffy duckling. With a quack and a kiss, Mama named her Feather.

Then wiggle, wobble . . .

CRACK!

Out hatched another duckling, flapping his wings.

With a quack and a kiss, Mama named him Flap.
"Look how big you both are," she said.

"I AM big," said Feather.
"I am full of bigness."

"I'm big, too!
    I'm big, too!" said Flap.

Feather fluffed herself up. "But I am bigger," she said.
"Now, now," said Mama. But the ducklings kept arguing.
They didn't notice that the last egg was rocking slowly.
Back and forth. Back and forth.

And he was.

With a quack and a kiss, Mama named him Spike.
Spike smiled at his sister and brother.
"Oh, what a sweet family," said Mama.

"I AM sweet," said Feather,
giving Mama a flower.
"I have oodles of sweetness."

"I'm sweet, too!

I'm sweet, too!" said Flap.

He handed Mama a whole bouquet.

"But I am sweeter," said Feather.

Mama giggled. "Oh, what a funny family."

"I AM funny!" cried Feather.
"I am bursting with funniness!"
She made a funny face.

She did a little dance.

She dove into the pond
with a splash.

"I'm funny, too!

I'm funny, too!" cried Flap.

"But I am funnier," said Feather.
And the ducklings kept arguing.

"I'm cold!" said Feather.
"I am shaking with coldness."

"I'm cold, too!
I'm cold, too!"
Flap shivered.

BRRRR!

"Oh, that won't do," said Mama.
"Who wants a cuddle?"

"I do," said Feather.

"I do, too! I do, too!" said Flap.

With a quack and three kisses, they cuddled together.
Under Mama's wings, no one was bigger,
or sweeter, or funnier, or better.

They were all the best.
The best family.